ICKYPOO

Written and Illustrated by Thomas Yu

Creative Footprints for Kids

LANDMARK HOUSE, LTD.—Midwest
1949 Foxridge Drive
Kansas City, KS 66106
913-722-0700

LANDMARK HOUSE, LTD.—Southwest
7047 East Greenway Pkwy.
Scottsdale, AZ 85254
480-659-4052

Dedicated to Mrs. Carolyn Walters, my third grade
teacher at Wyatt Elementary School and
Mrs. Minyi Kong, my art teacher, for their
guidance and inspiration.

To all my friends for their encouragement.
With special thanks to Angela Deng, for sharing her
knowledge and advice while I was creating my story.

And to my loving parents for making this wonderful
experience possible for me. Thank you!

First Printing

COPYRIGHT @ 2009 LANDMARK HOUSE, LTD.

Yu, Thomas, 1996 -

International Standard Book Number: 978-0-9822874-2-2 (lib. bdg.)

Midwest Branch
Landmark House, Ltd..
1949 Foxridge Drive
Kansas City, KS 66106
913-722-0700

Southwest Branch
Kierland Corporate Center
7047 East Greenway Parkway
Scottsdale, AZ 85254
480-659-4052

Printed in China

PANEL OF JUDGES

Deborah J. Ellis
Katie Lohmann
Dr. Adolph Moser
Jayna Miller-Schneider
Jon Goodall Symon
Scot Symon
Teresa M. Melton-Symon
Nancy R. Thatch-Melton

EDITORS
Deborah J. Ellis
Nancy Thatch Melton

ASSISTANT EDITOR
Allyson Alvarez

ART DIRECTOR
Jayna Miller-Schneider

RESEARCH
Teresa M. Melton-Symon

PRODUCTION CO-ORDINATOR
Eric Taylor
Four Colour Imports

PUBLISHER
LANDMARK HOUSE, LTD.

BOOK FORMATTING
Patricia Prather
Rodger McReynolds

FINANCIAL SUPPORTERS
J.G. Symon & Companies

ADVISORS
Justin Benster
Arthur Malcy
Jack Mandelbaum
Norman Polsky
Robert Regnier

FOUNDER
David Melton

Creative Footprints for Kids

NOTE FROM THE PUBLISHER

The publisher's letter about the student author and the book usually tells of the different mediums and techniques which the author used to create his or her book. This kind of information can be useful in helping the reader understand the artwork and text before them. Nevertheless, I would like to go a more personal route.

ICKYPOO came in to us under a completely different title — FREE CHAOS. The story and illustrations were exceptional. A close race ensued as to who would be Number One in the 6 – 9 age Category — but another book won. After contacting all of the respective winners and following several months, our eyes kept going back to Thomas Yu's wonderful book. It seemed to jump out at us every time we walked by the Contest Room.

Drawn to it the way that we were, a decision was finally made to offer him a PUBLISHER'S CHOICE GOLD AWARD. I phoned his parents and asked them if Thomas might be interested in letting us still publish his book in this special line and if he would mind working with us on the editing of his story and letting an art director guide him through improving his illustrations. Not only did he jump at the chance, but Thomas did not for one minute let us or himself down in refining his book.

For over a year, Thomas worked diligently to turn ICKYPOO into one of the most delightfully written and illustrated books by a child of his age. There is no doubt that Thomas has created an exceptional piece of literature accentuated by his colorfully fun artwork.

Please welcome to the literary scene the first national release of the young author/illustrator — Thomas Yu.

Enjoy your adventure in ICKYPOO!

TERESA M. MELTON-SYMON
President
Landmark House, Ltd.

P.S. Close to production time, the original 6 – 9 age category contest winner stepped aside making a personal decision not to have his book published. At that point, Thomas Yu — being the runner up — was moved into First Place.

Way out in the ocean was a small island called Ickypoo. Now Ickypoo was a peaceful place. And the people who lived there wanted to keep it that way. So they put up signs all around the island that read:

ICKYPOO
WORLD'S MOST PEACEFUL ISLAND
POPULATION 5000 PEACEFUL PEOPLE
NO RUDE VISITORS ALLOWED

All that peacefulness kept the Ickypooans very happy. Children went off to school happy. They were friendly and kind to everyone. Grown-ups went to work happy. They always worked hard and earned enough money to take good care of their families. All the pets in Ickypoo were happy, too. They were fed twice each day. Their bowls were kept full of nice, fresh water. They were taken on long walks. And each night, they were brought inside to sleep on soft, warm cushions.

The Ickypoo Pet Shop was one of the most popular places in town. It was usually filled with customers. It was always filled with more pets for sale. Mr. Fursmith, the owner of the shop, was really happy to sell pets to Ickypooans. He knew those pets would be going to good homes.

One afternoon, Mr. Fursmith heard a CLINK! CLINK! CLINK! "Something is hitting my roof!" he said in alarm. He hurried outside to take a look.

"OUCH! OUCH! OUCH!" he cried. "Now something is hitting my head!" When he looked up, he saw coins were falling all around him — silver coins! "Help!" he yelled. "Help! Help! Silver dollars are falling from the sky!"

His customers rushed outside. "OUCH! OW! OUCH! OW!" they cried and tried to cover their heads. They were amazed at what they saw. "Look at all of this money!" they shouted. "And it's FREE!"

They began scurrying about, grabbing as many silver dollars as they could. Men caught the coins in their hats. Women opened their purses. Children ran home and got their piggy banks. Everyone tried to find helmets for their heads. Mr. Fursmith simply grabbed an umbrella from his shop, turned it upside-down, and held it above his head.

Word spread quickly. Other Ickypooans came running. They brought pots and pans, buckets and baskets, flour sacks, milk pails, cash registers, wheelbarrows, and whatever else they could find.

For days and days, the coins kept falling, and the people kept catching them. In fact, that was all the people did. Children started skipping school. Grown ups quit their jobs. "After all," they said, "we are getting richer and richer. We do not need to work."

The rest of the world soon heard about Ickypoo's free money. The beaches of the island became clogged with boats of all kinds — ocean liners, yachts, steamboats, sailboats, motorboats, rowboats and even wooden rafts! There was no airport on the island, but even that didn't stop anyone. The skies of Ickypoo were soon filled with colorful hot-air balloons!

Then, things began to turn really bad.

Ickypoo was no longer a peaceful place. The PEACE signs were completely ignored, so they were soon torn down.

No one was happy. They were just greedy and rude. Cries of "Get out of my way! That money is mine!" were now heard more often than "Ow!" and "Ouch!"

Many people started pushing and shoving, and even fighting. Children became bullies. Best friends split up. Black eyes were seen everywhere. Doctors at Ickypoo Hospital worked day and night, just to set broken bones!

The pets were unhappy, too.

"My owner never feeds me on time!" snarled a cat.

"My owner never takes me for walks!" grumbled a monkey.

"My owner leaves me out in the cold all night!" growled a dog.

"It's not fair!" yelled another dog. "Let's leave here!"

"Yes, let's do that!" the others agreed.

And, one by one, the pets filed out of their homes and disappeared into the distance. That evening, the people of Ickypoo noticed that their pets were missing. They searched everywhere, but could not find them. Finally, they gave up and returned to their homes.

"It's just as well," one woman said, as she yawned and climbed into bed. "We are too busy getting rich. We really do not have time to take care of pets."

Then, something surprising happened. One morning, the silver dollars stopped falling from the sky. The people were very upset. They wanted more free money. So they kept watch for many months, but nothing happened.

"Never mind," the people finally said, "I suppose we are rich enough. Let's put our money in the bank where it will be safe."

Ickypoo began to settle down. All of the outsiders left the island. New PEACE signs were put up. And the children were sent back to school. However, the grown ups did not go back to work. They had become very lazy. All they wanted to do was sit around and count their silver dollars.

Mr. Goldbags, the owner of the Ickypoo Bank, didn't mind. He was happy to store all that money in his bank vault. He even set up a special room where the people could come and enjoy counting their coins.

One Friday afternoon, Mr. Goldbags and his secretary got ready to leave work. He was just putting on his hat when suddenly, he saw a dog sneak slowly behind a desk.

"What is that dog doing in here?" he called to her.

"Now, Mr. Goldbags, don't get excited," she replied with a smile. "There is no dog here. You know we never allow dogs in this bank."

He thought for a moment, then shrugged his shoulders. "Oh, well," he said, "I guess I just imagined it." He soon forgot all about the dog and left for a peaceful weekend.

But, when Mr. Goldbags returned on Monday, he was in for a big surprise. The bank lobby was filled with unhappy customers, including Mr. Fursmith. The people were really angry! They started yelling and screaming:

"My money is gone!"

"My money is gone, too!"

"What happened to our silver dollars?"

"The vault is almost empty!" they shouted. "Only a few bags of coins are left!"

"We think you stole our money!" Mr. Fursmith shouted.

"Oh! Oh! Oh! My goodness, NO!" Mr. Goldbags stammered. "I did not steal anything! Before I left last Friday, I locked all the doors and set the alarm."

"Well, somebody took our silver dollars!" snapped a woman. "And, what are you going to do about it?"

"I don't know," Mr. Goldbags replied, as he looked inside the vault and shook his head sadly.

"Let's talk to Mayor Busybody," suggested Mr. Fursmith. "He usually knows what to do."

"Yes!" everyone agreed. "Let's go to his office right now!"

Mayor Busybody was stunned when he heard the news. "We will need to find a good detective to investigate this robbery," he said. That very day, he hired one.

Mr. I Solvit arrived early the next morning. Everyone was waiting for him at the bank. The detective handed his business card to Mr. Goldbags. It read: MR. I. SOLVIT - SUPER SLEUTH

Mr. Solvit removed his hat. Then he opened his bag and took out a large magnifying glass.

"Where is your vault?" he asked in a businesslike tone. Mr. Goldbags led the way. Mr. Solvit followed close behind, kneeling now and then to pick up some tufts of black hair from the floor. "Hmmmm, this is very interesting," the detective said thoughtfully.

"What is it?" Mr. Goldbags asked.

"I believe it is hair from a dog." Mr. Solvit answered.

"Well, maybe I did see a dog in here after all," said Mr. Goldbags.

Mr. Solvit entered the vault and started looking around. "I also see some spots of dried saliva on these bags," he said.

"Are you saying that the thief drooled all over those bags?" a man asked.

"Oh, no. It was the dog that did the drooling."

"A drooling dog was in my bank?" Mr. Goldbags exclaimed.

"Maybe, and here is some more hair — brown hair. And over there are peanuts scattered all about."

"It looks as if the thief's drooling dog likes to eat peanuts," a woman said and giggled a bit.

"Absolutely not. This hair came from a monkey," replied Mr. Solvit.

"A monkey!" everyone gasped.

"Now we have a drooling dog and a hairy monkey!" grumbled Mr. Fursmith.

"Perhaps," answered Mr. Solvit, "but it was the monkey that ate the peanuts. There also are cat scratches on the wall, and over there, I see some feathers and birdseed."

"Nonsense!" remarked Mr. Goldbags, "I cannot believe that the thief had a cat with him, too — a cat that wore feathers and ate birdseed!"

Mr. Solvit did not bother to answer him. Instead, he requested that everyone leave the bank. "I just need peace and quiet to finish my investigation," he explained. "I also need to take fresh footprints and, oh, yes, paw prints, too," he chuckled.

"Well, just make sure you get our money back!" the crowd yelled.

"Do not worry," Mr. Solvit replied calmly. "I shall have this case solved by tomorrow."

After investigating the vault very carefully, the detective sat down to think about what he had found. He was still puzzled about the animals. "Why would a thief bring animals with him?" he wondered.

Then his experience in solving crimes began to give him some ideas. He remembered that thieves sometimes rob the same place twice. And there were still some bags of coins left. That meant, the thief might return to finish the robbery. "Yes!" he exclaimed. "I think the thief will be back! And I — Mr. I. Solvit, super sleuth, am going to set a trap for him!"

That night, Mr. Solvit hid behind a door in the bank. With the lights turned low, no one could see him. He waited, and he watched. Nothing moved. Except for the ticking of a grandfather clock, the bank was completely silent.

Then, just as the clock struck midnight, a huge chandelier began to sway back and forth, and back and forth. In a few minutes, something crawled out of it and stayed hidden near the ceiling.

Mr. Solvit's heart began to beat faster. He could not see exactly what was up there. But, whatever it was, it was BIG!

Finally, that something swung down out of the shadows. Now Mr. Solvit could see it. It was a MONKEY — a big monkey!

The animal stood there and looked around a few minutes. Then it hurried over to a desk and sat down. After entering a few computer codes, the monkey quickly hacked into the alarm system and turned it off.

Mr. Solvit was shocked at what he had just seen!

The monkey was pleased with what it had just done!

It chattered happily to itself. Then it climbed on top of the computer, proudly stuck out its chest, and gave a long, low whistle.

Now Mr. Solvit was really shocked! All kinds of animals started popping out from hiding places! They came down from the ceiling. They raced up from the basement. They crawled from under desks, crept from behind doors, and jumped out of drawers and trash cans.

Mr. Solvit watched as the animals hurried to the vault. They gathered up the rest of the bags, carried them outside, and loaded them onto a wagon.

"So that's how it was done," the detective said to himself. "That thief has trained his animals well. They can actually rob a bank for him! What a smart way to hide his own identity. It is clear that I am dealing with a clever thief. But, I have never failed to solve a case, and I will not fail this time!"

When all the animals had left, Mr. Solvit slipped out a side door and followed the wagon. He stayed far enough back, so no one would see him.

After a few miles, the wagon was stopped at the mouth of a cave. The animals quickly unloaded the bags and carried them inside.

"Ah, yes," Mr. Solvit said to himself. "This must be their hideout. Their leader will probably be here, too, and I will arrest him!"

Before long, the detective began following the animals. Deeper and deeper, he went into the cave. When he came to a large cavern, he stopped. Then he crept closer for a better look. "What is happening?" he said to himself. "I see no person here. I see only animals!"

After a while, Mr. Solvit stepped out from the shadows. "What is going on here?" he demanded to know. "Where did you come from? And where is your leader?"

For a few moments, all the animals froze in fear. The cats stopped playing in the silver dollars. The dogs stopped chewing on the coins. The birds stopped chirping. The monkeys stopped chattering and jumping about.

Mr. Solvit looked all around. He recognized the monkey that had hacked into the alarm system. "Speak up!" he said loudly, as he stared directly at the animal.

Finally, the monkey stepped forward. "We are the pets from Ickypoo," it said in a trembling voice. "We have no leader. We are alone."

Mr. Solvit had to admit that he was surprised. "Then you are the ones that planned the robbery!" he exclaimed. "How smart you are. But, why? Why did you decide to rob the bank?"

"Because our owners had become too greedy," the monkey explained. "They were so busy catching silver dollars that they forgot all about taking good care of us."

Now Mr. Solvit understood what the animals had tried to do. "Without all that money," he said, "you hoped your owners would start giving more attention to you."

"That's right!" meowed a cat, and the others voiced their agreement.

"Well, the people were wrong to be so greedy," Mr. Solvit told them. "However, you were just as wrong to steal the money. You must return that money right away."

"We are willing to do that," said the monkey. "But first, the people must agree to our deal."

"And what is that deal?" the detective wanted to know.

The monkey hopped up on Mr. Solvit's shoulder and started whispering in his ear.

As the detective listened, he began to smile. Then he began to chuckle. And then he laughed and patted the monkey on the back.

"I understand exactly what you are telling me," he said. "And I'll make sure everyone else understands your deal, too."

The very next morning, Mr. Solvit stood before the people of Ickypoo. After he explained about the robbery, everyone shouted, "Hooray! Hooray! We can have our money back and our pets back, too!"

"Not so fast," Mr. Solvit said. "I must tell you one more thing. Before your pets will agree to return the money, they insist upon making a deal with you."

"A deal!" everyone grumbled. "We do not have to make a deal with animals — especially our own pets!"

"I'm afraid you do," Mr. Solvit replied firmly.

"Okay, okay," sighed Mayor Busybody. "I suppose it's always best to make a deal. Exactly what kind of deal is it?"

Mr. Solvit looked sternly at the people and said, "The deal is: You can have your money back, or you can have your pets back. You cannot have both."

It did not take long for the grown-ups to make a choice. "We'll take the money!" they yelled.

"Stop!" said the children. "Stop right now! We have not voted yet. And all of us have decided that we want our pets back!"

The arguments lasted several hours. No one could agree. Then, one small boy spoke up: "My pet and I are pals. Where he goes, I go. And where I go, he goes."

The other children agreed. They shouted: "Now you have to deal with us, too.
And our deal is this: NO PETS, NO CHILDREN!
If we do not get our pets back, we will leave home at once!"

"Oh, no!" the grown-ups exclaimed. "We love our children. We cannot let them go!"

"Okay," Mayor Busybody finally said, "Let's be reasonable. Maybe it would be best if we gave up the money."

"Yes," most of the grown-ups agreed. "That money has already caused us too much trouble."

"But, what will we do with all of those silver dollars?" Mr. Goldbags wondered.

"GIVE THEM TO THE ICKYPOO HUMANE SOCIETY!" the children shouted. And that's exactly what they did.

Everyone was happy.

Mr. Solvit was happy, too. He had solved another case!

All of the Ickypooans thanked him. And if you ever visit the island of Ickypoo, you will see a statue of the detective. It stands in the center of the town square. The words at the base read:

MR. I. SOLVIT - SUPER SLEUTH
HE BROUGHT PEACE BACK TO ICKYPOO!

Creative Footprints for Kids

LANDMARK HOUSE, LTD.